Braves™

Take Me Out To The Ballgame™

Julie Parker

Illustrated by Jon Chad

www.mascotbooks.com

It was a beautiful day in Atlanta, Georgia. Bobby and his dad were outside playing catch when Bobby had an idea. "Take me to the Braves game, Dad!" said Bobby. "That is a great idea! I bet your sister, Maggie, and your mom will want to come, too. Let's go!" said Mr. Jones.

"Look, there's Turner Field. We're here!" said Bobby.
Mr. Jones parked their car in the Green Lot, right near
the spot where Hank Aaron hit his 715th home run at
old Atlanta Fulton County Stadium. As they walked
toward Turner Field, they saw Braves fans along the
way. The fans yelled, "Go, Braves!" They walked along
Hank Aaron Boulevard on their way to the stadium.

"Do you see the statue of Hank Aaron?" asked Mr. Jones. "He sure was a great baseball player. Some people called him "Hammerin' Hank" because he hit so many home runs. He is a true hero and an Atlanta Braves legend."

"Can we paint our faces and play in Tooner Field?
Please, please, please?" Bobby and Maggie asked.

The Jones family headed toward Tooner Field,
and along the way, they cheered, "Let's go, Braves!"

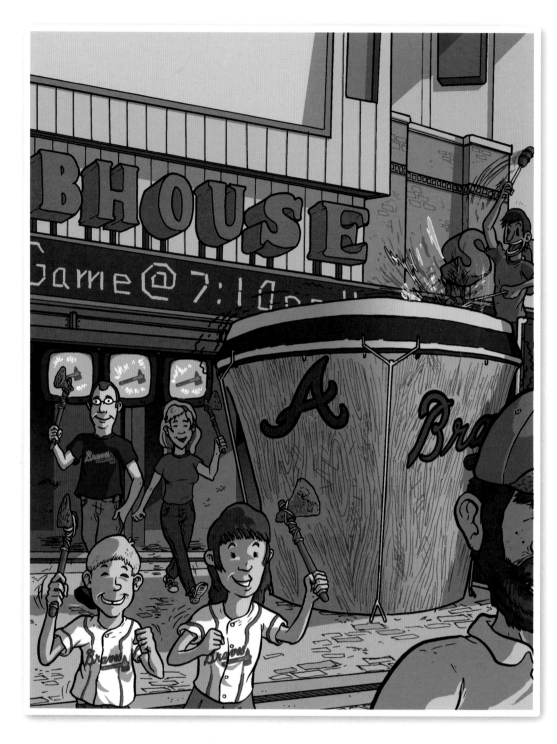

"I hear someone beating on the big Braves drum! We need to get ready for the game! Let's get a tomahawk from the Club House! Can you do the Tomahawk Chop?" asked Mr. Jones. "Whooa whoa whoawa whooa whoa whoa whoawa whooa!" they yelled as they chopped their tomahawks back and forth.

The Jones family headed for their seats.

Can you point to the batting helmet,
batting gloves, bat, cleats, and jersey?

"Let's watch batting practice," said Maggie.
"Look, the baseball players have on their uniforms."

"Heads up, it's a foul ball! You caught it, Dad!
We are so lucky!" exclaimed Maggie. "Here comes
the baseball player. He is going to autograph our
baseball!" The Jones family loved coming early to
watch batting practice.

See the pitcher wind-up as he delivers a fastball!

Mrs. Jones pointed to another Braves baseball player. "Look over there," she said. "Do you see the pitcher? He's warming up his arm."

Fans all around them chanted, "Let's go, Braves! Let's go, Braves!"

O! say can you see by the dawn's early light
What so proudly we hailed at the twilight's last gleaming.
Whose broad stripes and bright stars through the perilous fight,
O'er the ramparts we watched were so gallantly streaming.
And the rockets' red glare, the bombs bursting in air,
Gave proof through the night that our flag was still there.
O! say does that star-spangled banner yet wave
O'er the land of the free
and the home of the brave?

Can you sing along?

"The game is about to start. Everyone is taking off their hats and standing up. Get ready to sing the National Anthem!" said Mrs. Jones.

Can you point to the 1st , 2nd, and 3rd basemen? Can you point to the catcher, shortstop, outfielders, and umpire?

The umpire yelled, "Play Ball!" to start the game. Nine Braves players sprinted onto the field and took their positions. Bobby's favorite player was the shortstop. Maggie liked the first baseman. Mrs. Jones liked the center fielder. Mr. Jones was a fan of the manager.

After the visitors finished batting, the first Braves batter stepped up to the plate. On the second pitch, he hit the ball deep into the outfield and hustled around the bases. With a messy slide, he touched home plate before the catcher tagged him with the ball. He was safe! The Braves hit an inside-the-park home run! Go, Braves!

"I want to run the bases too, Dad!" said Maggie.
"We can! Let's go to Sky Field!" said Dad. Everyone headed toward the escalator—all the way to the top of the stadium by the big cola bottle!

Mr. Jones explained to Maggie and Bobby that the famous cola bottle at Turner Field was made with 60 shoes, 2,000 bottle caps, 48 batting helmets, 2,000 cans, 18 catcher's mitts, 86 fielder's gloves, 290 bats, 6,680 baseballs, 24 jerseys, 64 bases, 16 chest protectors, and 24 pitching rubbers. Bobby and Maggie were impressed!

Bobby and Maggie imagined themselves as real
Atlanta Braves baseball players. They ran around
the bases as fast as they could. "Run the bases!
Go, Bobby! Go, Maggie! You're safe! Let's do it again!"
said Mrs. Jones. The kids had fun, but it surely was tiring!

After running around, Maggie and Bobby were hungry. Fortunately, the concession stand was right around the corner. The kids loaded up on hot dogs, popcorn, and drinks. "Yummy!" said Mrs. Jones. "Hurry! We don't want to miss the seventh inning stretch."

The Jones family and all of the baseball fans sang *Take Me Out to the Ballgame*, arm in arm.

"That was fun!" said Bobby. "Wow, look! We are on the big screen. Wave hello!" The Jones family waved to all their friends at Turner Field.

At the end of the eighth inning, Bobby and Maggie watched as the Braves made their way back to the team's dugout. The Braves players were cheering for their teammates and encouraging each other.

In the bottom of the ninth inning, the Braves were down to their last at-bat. The game was tied. The bases were loaded. There were two outs. The Braves batter swung with all his might and hit the ball deep into the night sky. HOME RUN! A GRAND SLAM! **BRAVES WIN, BRAVES WIN,** *BRAVES WIN!* The crowd cheered for the home team. Overhead, colorful fireworks erupted.

"That was the best game I've ever seen!" said
Bobby. "Thanks for bringing us!" said Maggie.
"Goodbye!" said the Jones family to the Braves
mascot. "See y'all next time!" replied the mascot.

When the Jones family arrived back home, everyone was tired after the exciting day at Turner Field. Bobby and Maggie went straight to bed. "Good night, Bobby. Good night, Maggie. Love you both!" Mr. and Mrs. Jones said as they tucked them in for the night. As the children drifted off to sleep, they thought, "Go, Braves."

For Wiley and Ben. ~ Julie Parker

Dedicated to books on tape; perfect for a guy who's
too busy drawing children's books! ~ Jon Chad
www.jonchad.com

For more information about our products,
please visit us online at www.mascotbooks.com.

For more information, please contact Mascot Books,
P.O. Box 220157, Chantilly, VA 20153-0157

ISBN: 0-692000-41-0

Printed in the United States.

Baseball

Boston Red Sox	Hello, *Wally*!	Jerry Remy
Boston Red Sox	*Wally The Green Monster And His Journey Through Red Sox Nation!*	Jerry Remy
Boston Red Sox	Coast to Coast with *Wally The Green Monster*	Jerry Remy
Boston Red Sox	A Season with *Wally The Green Monster*	Jerry Remy
Colorado Rockies	Hello, *Dinger*!	Aimee Aryal
Detroit Tigers	Hello, *Paws*!	Aimee Aryal
New York Yankees	Let's Go, *Yankees*!	Yogi Berra
New York Yankees	*Yankees* Town	Aimee Aryal
New York Mets	Hello, *Mr. Met*!	Rusty Staub
New York Mets	*Mr. Met* and his Journey Through the Big Apple	Aimee Aryal
St. Louis Cardinals	Hello, *Fredbird*!	Ozzie Smith
Philadelphia Phillies	Hello, *Phillie Phanatic*!	Aimee Aryal
Chicago Cubs	Let's Go, *Cubs*!	Aimee Aryal
Chicago White Sox	Let's Go, *White Sox*!	Aimee Aryal
Cleveland Indians	Hello, *Slider*!	Bob Feller
Seattle Mariners	Hello, *Mariner Moose*!	Aimee Aryal
Washington Nationals	Hello, *Screech*!	Aimee Aryal
Milwaukee Brewers	Hello, *Bernie Brewer*!	Aimee Aryal

College

Alabama	Hello, Big Al!	Aimee Aryal
Alabama	Roll Tide!	Ken Stabler
Alabama	Big Al's Journey Through the Yellowhammer State	Aimee Aryal
Arizona	Hello, Wilbur!	Lute Olson
Arizona State	Hello, Sparky!	Aimee Aryal
Arkansas	Hello, Big Red!	Aimee Aryal
Arkansas	Big Red's Journey Through the Razorback State	Aimee Aryal
Auburn	Hello, Aubie!	Aimee Aryal
Auburn	War Eagle!	Pat Dye
Auburn	Aubie's Journey Through the Yellowhammer State	Aimee Aryal
Boston College	Hello, Baldwin!	Aimee Aryal
Brigham Young	Hello, Cosmo!	LaVell Edwards
Cal - Berkeley	Hello, Oski!	Aimee Aryal
Clemson	Hello, Tiger!	Aimee Aryal
Clemson	Tiger's Journey Through the Palmetto State	Aimee Aryal
Colorado	Hello, Ralphie!	Aimee Aryal
Connecticut	Hello, Jonathan!	Aimee Aryal
Duke	Hello, Blue Devil!	Aimee Aryal
Florida	Hello, Albert!	Aimee Aryal
Florida	Albert's Journey Through the Sunshine State	Aimee Aryal
Florida State	Let's Go, 'Noles!	Aimee Aryal
Georgia	Hello, Hairy Dawg!	Aimee Aryal
Georgia	How 'Bout Them Dawgs!	Vince Dooley
Georgia	Hairy Dawg's Journey Through the Peach State	Vince Dooley
Georgia Tech	Hello, Buzz!	Aimee Aryal
Gonzaga	Spike, The Gonzaga Bulldog	Mike Pringle
Illinois	Let's Go, Illini!	Aimee Aryal
Indiana	Let's Go, Hoosiers!	Aimee Aryal
Iowa	Hello, Herky!	Aimee Aryal
Iowa State	Hello, Cy!	Amy DeLashmutt
James Madison	Hello, Duke Dog!	Aimee Aryal
Kansas	Hello, Big Jay!	Aimee Aryal
Kansas State	Hello, Willie!	Dan Walter
Kentucky	Hello, Wildcat!	Aimee Aryal
LSU	Hello, Mike!	Aimee Aryal
LSU	Mike's Journey Through the Bayou State	Aimee Aryal
Maryland	Hello, Testudo!	Aimee Aryal
Michigan	Let's Go, Blue!	Aimee Aryal
Michigan State	Hello, Sparty!	Aimee Aryal
Michigan State	Sparty's Journey Through Michigan	Aimee Aryal
Middle Tennessee	Hello, Lightning!	Aimee Aryal
Minnesota	Hello, Goldy!	Aimee Aryal
Mississippi	Hello, Colonel Rebel!	Aimee Aryal

Pro Football

Carolina Panthers	Let's Go, Panthers!	Aimee Aryal
Chicago Bears	Let's Go, Bears!	Aimee Aryal
Dallas Cowboys	How 'Bout Them Cowboys!	Aimee Aryal
Green Bay Packers	Go, Pack, Go!	Aimee Aryal
Kansas City Chiefs	Let's Go, Chiefs!	Aimee Aryal
Minnesota Vikings	Let's Go, Vikings!	Aimee Aryal
New York Giants	Let's Go, Giants!	Aimee Aryal
New York Jets	J-E-T-S! Jets, Jets, Jets!	Aimee Aryal
New England Patriots	Let's Go, Patriots!	Aimee Aryal
Pittsburg Steelers	Here We Go, Steelers!	Aimee Aryal
Seattle Seahawks	Let's Go, Seahawks!	Aimee Aryal
Washington Redskins	Hail To The Redskins!	Aimee Aryal

Basketball

Dallas Mavericks	Let's Go, Mavs!	Mark Cuban
Boston Celtics	Let's Go, Celtics!	Aimee Aryal

Other

Kentucky Derby	White Diamond Runs For The Roses	Aimee Aryal
Marine Corps Marathon	Run, Miles, Run!	Aimee Aryal
Mississippi State	Hello, Bully!	Aimee Aryal
Missouri	Hello, Truman!	Todd Donoho
Missouri	Hello, Truman! Show Me Missouri!	Todd Donoho
Nebraska	Hello, Herbie Husker!	Aimee Aryal
North Carolina	Hello, Rameses!	Aimee Aryal
North Carolina	Rameses' Journey Through the Tar Heel State	Aimee Aryal
North Carolina St.	Hello, Mr. Wuf!	Aimee Aryal
North Carolina St.	Mr. Wuf's Journey Through North Carolina	Aimee Aryal
Northern Arizona	Hello, Louie!	Jeanette S. Baker
Notre Dame	Let's Go, Irish!	Aimee Aryal
Ohio State	Hello, Brutus!	Aimee Aryal
Ohio State	Brutus' Journey	Aimee Aryal
Oklahoma	Let's Go, Sooners!	Aimee Aryal
Oklahoma State	Hello, Pistol Pete!	Aimee Aryal
Oregon	Go Ducks!	Aimee Aryal
Oregon State	Hello, Benny the Beaver!	Aimee Aryal
Penn State	Hello, Nittany Lion!	Aimee Aryal
Penn State	We Are Penn State!	Joe Paterno
Purdue	Hello, Purdue Pete!	Aimee Aryal
Rutgers	Hello, Scarlet Knight!	Aimee Aryal
South Carolina	Hello, Cocky!	Aimee Aryal
South Carolina	Cocky's Journey Through the Palmetto State	Aimee Aryal
So. California	Hello, Tommy Trojan!	Aimee Aryal
Syracuse	Hello, Otto!	Aimee Aryal
Tennessee	Hello, Smokey!	Aimee Aryal
Tennessee	Smokey's Journey Through the Volunteer State	Aimee Aryal
Texas	Hello, Hook 'Em!	Aimee Aryal
Texas	Hook 'Em's Journey Through the Lone Star State	Aimee Aryal
Texas A & M	Howdy, Reveille!	Aimee Aryal
Texas A & M	Reveille's Journey Through the Lone Star State	Aimee Aryal
Texas Tech	Hello, Masked Rider!	Aimee Aryal
UCLA	Hello, Joe Bruin!	Aimee Aryal
Virginia	Hello, CavMan!	Aimee Aryal
Virginia Tech	Hello, Hokie Bird!	Aimee Aryal
Virginia Tech	Yea, It's Hokie Game Day!	Frank Beamer
Virginia Tech	Hokie Bird's Journey Through Virginia	Aimee Aryal
Wake Forest	Hello, Demon Deacon!	Aimee Aryal
Washington	Hello, Harry the Husky!	Aimee Aryal
Washington State	Hello, Butch!	Aimee Aryal
West Virginia	Hello, Mountaineer!	Aimee Aryal
West Virginia	The Mountaineer's Journey Through West Virginia	Leslie H. Haning
Wisconsin	Hello, Bucky!	Aimee Aryal
Wisconsin	Bucky's Journey Through the Badger State	Aimee Aryal